AF265304

REFLECTIONS

Anthologies of Lewis Wamwanda
(2019)

No part of this publication may be stored in retrieve form, reproduced or transmitted in any form or by any means of electronic, mechanical, photocopying or otherwise without prior written permission of the publisher.
Short extracts may be used for review purpose

Copyright © Lewis Wamwanda 2019

LULU PRESS, INC.
Lulu.com

ISBN 978-0-359-91977-2

CONTACTS
lewamwanda@gmail.com

ACKNOWLEDGEMENT

I would like to acknowledge my mentor Dr. Christopher Okemwa who inspired and encouraged me to write poetry. I won't forget Dr. Imali Abala for offering me moral support. I can't forget to mention Margaret Wairimu, Angiey Pajero, Dorothy Nyandega, Esther Andaye, Hellen Kironji, Chrismoh Maobe and my Friend Cliff Oyugi for inspiring me and being my number one fans. All in all everything couldn't have been made possible without the grace of the Almighty God.

My gratitude to all of you who made **REFLECTIONS** a success.

DEDICATION

I dedicate this Anthology to these men who stood by me, my dad Bishop Ellam Wamwanda, Brother Lazarus Wamwanda and Brother Ezekiel Immo
To the greatest women in my life, My mum Elizabeth Immo, Mum Salome Wawire, To my sisters, Beatrice Lusike, Rael Naova and Gladys Wamwanda
And Finally to Ashley Kuntai, The woman I love

TABLE OF CONTENTS

TEAR DROP

Tears of the past days
Forgotten by time,
Assumed by many
Fear to remember the past
But still she feels the pain

She went to school, yes
She did her primary level, yes
She passed, they say, yes
But she was a girl, not a child
And had to go, and bring cows

She tried to voice her sound,
To scream for help
To beg for a chance
A chance to schooling
A girl, how can anyone hear?

Now she is twenty
And a dozen of off springs
With a drunk man
Empty plates on the table
Twenty four eyes looking at her
But no one dares to speak

Her memories linger six years back
A mere, bright, hardworking girl
A bright anticipated future
A good and rich husband
But all she got now,
A tear drop to wipe

MY LOVE FOR YOU

In the depths of my heart,
Lay some investments,
Intangible investments,
Unseen things,
That all belong to one person.....

Many wish for these but very few make it,
Many trust their partners but it all goes to waste,
Many love them but the aftermath of all these are heartbreaks....

A broken heart cannot speak,
It cannot beat normally,
It cannot function properly,
The result of this becomes terrible

In you I found true love,
The word love brought meaning to me,
In my heart lie my feelings for you,
I love you more than words can explain.

They say to the moon and back,
But for ours I can't tell,
The respect you have accorded unto me made me love you even more,
You are handsome and you know that,
You have a glowing heart...

My pen cannot describe it all,
My words may not be sufficient,
To explain the feelings I have for you,
I just hope that you'll be mine forever,
That not even the grave can do us part,
Because we'll rest together.

All I just wanted you to know,
Is that my blood vessels squeezed themselves,
Just to create a perfect room for my better half....

Am out of ink,
Let me rest my case here,
But just know,
Just keep in mind that I treasure you

WE DIED YESTERDAY

Like an ox pulling a wagon
Sweating and breathing
Moaning at the load behind
Are our minds, tired and wasted

We believe in making a better tomorrow
And perfecting a remaining today
Forgetting the fight of yesterday
That killed the better half of ours

We claim to be heroes,
Fought and won our freedom
But a lie it is, we fear to face
For yesterday, we fought and died

Freedom is happiness
Happiness is love
Love is for the chosen few
We, the rest, killed by our burdens

We watch silently,
As they kill our remains
We cry tearlessly
For the tears were wasted yesterday

We died yesterday,
As we struggled for freedom
Not seen, not felt
We died yesterday.

OUR SHARE

We fought for freedom
To eat of its fruits together
To dance at its music together
Yet our fight is in vein

We shaded a lot of blood
Our brothers and sisters gone
For us to eat together of the fruit

You turned to pigs
Greedy, angry and hungry
A chameleon you changed
Grabbing all our toils
And leaving us in the cold

Give us our share
Equally, with no bias
Put down your weapons
Hold our hands, and let's eat together

Ours is to preach peace
Claiming our rights
Our father's wealth
Our soil, our land

We speak for the weak
We speak what is right
See, we fought together
The token we share equally

I, the spokesman
In peace and love
Not begging or demanding
But claiming for ours

I WANT TO WRITE

I want to write
And voice my thoughts
But a problem I have
Know not how to write

I want to write
A letter to my love
A letter of love
But I have no hands

I still want to write
A long letter of expressions
Of happiness and joy
But I got no paper

In this dungeon
Full of rats and filth
Strong dark iron bars
No paper within reach

I want to write a letter
To my wife and children
To apologize for mine deeds
And beg for their mercies

I want to write a letter
Giving reasons to my family
To tell them of the fateful day
That gave a free ride
To this dungeon of mine

I want to write a letter
But my hands are no more
Beaten by the rocks in the mines
Cut by the pebbles in the mines
I want to write a letter
And warn all out their
To play by their cards
And not fall prey of the blue men

I want to write a letter
But I have no pen
Papers are not available
And the bell has rang

I want to write a letter
But I have to run to parade
And manage to escape a few painful whips
And to lengthen my stay in the world.

LIFE IS A SCAM

We struggle to keep running
Holding on to tomorrow
But the tags we carry
Threatens to pull us back to yesterday

They say life is fair
I have no prove on that
For mine has not flowed their way
Difference is the momentum

We struggle for bread
Yet on our tables are crumbs
We struggle for a little wine
All we get is a drop of water

Life
Life is unfair
We work at the same work
But why do they get richer?
And me?
Poorer by passing seconds

We cry and sweat
Toiling all day long
They dine and laugh
Making merry all day

Life is a scam
A witness I am
And will fight
Till end of time

GOODBYE LOVE

I never meant to lie
For I wanted to keep you
I wanted to lose you not
Hence kept lying

How could I say the truth?
Without risking your leave?
Truth hurts, more than stings
How could I?

How could I say am poor?
And can't take care of you
Let alone our baby
And I had to lie

I wasn't meant to steal
But you had to eat
You had to clothe
And above all to be happy

You left me alone
When the truth you heard
And my mind was blurred
Taking the pill was my option

I cannot leave without you
And in death found solace
Don't come to my burial
Because my body won't withstand your tears

Tell Natalia, daddy loves her
I will be watching with the moon
For I failed her
And you the most

IT WAS NOT MY FAULT

Mama, why did this
Mama, I was to be your hope
Your happiness and life
It was not my fault

Mama, was I even there?
When grandma talked to you
Warned you of the bastard?
My unseen papa

Mama, I wasn't there
The moon was there though
Watching with shame,
The crickets chirped with sorrow
As you devoured the forbidden
You were not ashamed,
When thorns pricked your bare back
And your screams rented the air
In the name of love

Now I suffer the fate of your mistake
In this cold dark dungeon
Cursing and crying
Tearless, voiceless cries

Mama, I was to be your first
And maybe the last
But you broke the bridge
And snatched my temporal home

I won't see the sun
I won't be bathed with moon's love
You killed an innocent
It was not my fault

DEAR GOD OF HEAVEN

Dear God of heaven,
I don't know how to pray
But a few words from my mouth
May show the wants of my heart

I'm not worth to pray
But see, God my neighbor has a wife
I'm not lustful at all
But I pray if given a chance
I will treat her better than him

Dear God of heaven
If my answers are given
I promise to change my drinking habits
From drinking five bottles a week
To drinking three bottles a day

Dear God of heaven,
I'm not selfish as many say
Try and give me wealth
And all the beggars in town
Will be happily eating crumbs at my doorstep

Dear God of heaven,
I'm not an adulterer at all
All I pray to you father
Give me two or three women today
To prove to my loving wife
And the neighbors at our home
I'm still good in bed

Dear God of heaven
When my answers will be answered
I promise to go to church
During the weddings of saints
And parties of the church
My generosity will be seen
As I supply free booze to saints

FROM MY CHAINS

I was a good child to my parents
A good example to my friend's parents
Mark mine words
"I was"

Am dying from self-denial
For am chocking from within
And the chains holding me are heavy
But my desires hold me away from salvation

I want to stop it
I wish to stop
But I fail
Am weak and a coward

I am a slave of addiction
A slave of drugs and drinks
From a sip to sips
A puff to puffs
Slowly leading to my grave

My will I write
To the youths all right
My advice to heed
Don't fall a prey
And a drinking one to be

Am dying from drinking
Poison and death
Dirt and immoral
Yet I can't stop
Yet I can't.

GIVE ME A YEAR

Give me a year, just one.
Give me a year to prove mine worth,
Give me a year to serve the nation,
And fulfill my Promises.

Give me a year my people,
I will build all those bridges,
And I promise to Increase your wedges,
From fifty a day, to a hundred a week.

Give me a year my friends,
To serve you well,
To sack all the corrupt
And for a small fee from you
To give out free jobs for all

It's only a year, only one,
To bring change to you,
Free education, tax free nation,
Give me a year

COME BACK DADA (SISTER)

I don't know why they dug a hole
Put you in a big wooden box
And covered you in soil
I still don't know why

But dada, since papa took you
In that red crying vehicle
Mama has never been the same
She cried like me, when I was young
Sometimes I laughed at her
Sometimes I cried with her

I have a lot to tell you sister
I know you are down there
But when I finish digging this mound
I will take you out
And tell you of what you missed

First we have to kill them all
Who kept you on the box?
And covered you dip with soil
I personally have five cents in my pockets
And together we will buy big boxes for them

Dada, come back home,
People say you died,
Thinking I'm a fool to believe
But didn't I see?
When mama cried? And papa never dared to look at me
As those men in black
With ropes lowering you down the deep hole
I saw, and one day, we will avenge

Listen dada, I will come tomorrow and dig again
For now I have to go
For mama warned me of coming here
And I don't want to see her sad again
Since she rarely smiles since you went

But promise me dada,
If I dig this mound
You will come back home
And make mama smile
And papa to stop drinking

ALONE

You won't understand either,
So I seize to talk.
Call me a coward,
Or perhaps proud
But my pain, won't understand

Blooding is oozing
Pain inflicted in me
Yet I say I'm ok
And pretend to put a smile

Sometimes we laugh,
Making jokes until late
Drinking and eating
But I still feel alone

I wish to die
Slow, painless death
Deep down in my sleep
To wake up and see myself dead

Not to talk,
Not to laugh
Not to cry
Silence!

But these are just illusions
Chains of loneliness holding me
Tightly breaking my soul
Forcing my inner to give in

If only you could understand,
And feel my pain
And bare my pains
Then the world apart
Will be one whole ball

They celebrate when the sun rises
Yet my burden of sadness increases
My sack of pain becomes heavier
With lots of condemnations
Lots of judgments.

Am alone

I DON'T WANT TO

I don't want to be lazy
I fear the poverty blaze
The poverty terrifying memories
Cannot allow me to be at ease
To me I want it to be a tale
To my family hard work I will tell.

Not because of pride
But the honor I want
The status I want
Not to sit down, at the pavements
Beaten and bitten by cold
Stretching my hand for a coin

I don't want to be lazy
And wake up after sunset
Tired by the rumbling of the stomach
And the aching soles from yesterday's strolls
In search of coins from the rich
Or odd jobs on the reach

I don't want to be lazy
For my fear of poverty
Drives me by day
And keeps me awake till dawn
To accomplish those dreams
And be rich tomorrow

I have a tale to tell
An example to be
My family to be proud
My dad to stand up at the community
My mama to be respected at the village well
And men and women of the society
To be proud of their son

THINGS I LOVE ABOUT YOU

Not your wealth or your status,
But the smiles on your face,
The eyes that burns with love,
The lips that speak of love
These are the things I Love.

The honesty you possess,
And the kindness seen in you.
All mould to character.
These are just but a few,
Of the things I love about you.

The things I love about you,
That at times drives me insane,
Or perhaps mad, as they say,
Is the love you possess?
That warms the hearts of many.

The things I love about you,
Can fill hundreds of pages,
Take me a hundred years,
And my pen runs dry,
If I write of them all.

WHAT IS LOVE?

Tell me what love is,
Is it that feeling of attraction between two people?
Or just having lustful feelings,
Is it just a word?
That people play around with,
Is it just a game?
With sex as a goal,

I thought love is that feeling,
Of being comfortable in one's presence,
Having your best moments in one's silence,
A sense of belonging in one's life,
Emptiness when missing someone,

I wish in love,
I will breathe in peace, and cast the pain away,
I will heal my brokenness and feel myself whole,
I will not be afraid of getting hurt again,
I will have a voice and not only follow orders,

Hope to love and be loved back,
That true love from an honest person,
I wish to enjoy the fruits of love
The sweet fruits of love
Tell me, what is love?

YESTERDAY

I was sitting just outside the gate
Watching the birds return home happily
And the cold breeze biting my black cold skin
And the sky turning black with dark

So yesterday, I was sitting just outside the gate
Watching the white children of our neighbors
Playing and laughing happily
And the sky turned black with dark

So yesterday, I was sitting just outside the gate
Shivering with cold, from the teasing cold breeze
As I watched Mama Peter cooking Maandazi
And the breeze carried the aroma
Right through my nostrils

So yesterday, I was sitting just outside the gate
Watching silently at the passers by
Laughing and jeering at the boy outside the gate
Shivering with cold, angry and hungry
And the sky grew dark with dusk

So yesterday, I was sitting just outside the gate
Watching the dogs at the nearby bins
Fighting and rumbling over leftovers
And I swallowed deeply my saliva
And shifted my eyes on the other side of the road

So yesterday, I was sitting just outside the gate
As the last birds sung their last
And the playing children ran to their homes
And Mama Peter sold her last maandazi
And the last passer by passed me
And the dogs stopped fighting
And I shifted myself
And leaned on the gate
To try and catch some sleep.

MINE WAS NOT LOVE

The fact that we met and talked
The phone calls we made 'till late nights
Laughing till dawn catches up
Does not mean love to me

I smile when we meet
Yearning for the next visit
And the still moments we are together
Happily listening to your unending stories
But still, it does not mean love

Those late nights we spend together
And the long weekend gateways
To the woods and the oceans
And the frequent parties
Does not mean that I Love

Those tears that I wipe
When you are low and sad
Taking you by my arms
And resting in my comforting hugs
Still does not mean that I Love

That special visit to pa and ma
And when everyone said you are good
And praised you all day long
And talked about you being a good wife
Does not explain of love to me

The jumper I made you wear
During that chilly walk at the beach
And I shivered by from the sea breeze
Making my skin cold and numb
Still, does not explain about Love

WHAT LOVE IS, TO ME

The fact that we don't talk daily
And even rarely meet
Or laugh all night long
Does not mean I don't love

The fact that we don't go out
And prefer to cook at home
Wash utensils, and do the cleaning
Means Love to me

The fact that we have busy schedules
From dawn to dawn, dusk to dusk
And pause a second to say hi
Or a moment to say goodnight
Means love to me

The fact that you cry when I cry
And travel miles to be a comfort
And travel miles to give a hug
And tears to wipe
Means love to me

The fact that we fight all night
And wake up in the morning to smile
To laugh and talk happily
And not remembering about yesterday
Means love to me

The fact that you choose to miss the bus
And choose to push me to town
Not because you have no money
But because I have no limbs
Means love to me

The fact that you miss all those CATS
Just to take me on my frequent check ups
And volunteer to push my wheelchair
Assuming the preying eyes
Means Love to me

The fact that you take sign language classes
And learn to talk to me in signs
And patiently willing to learn
And your time offering whole
Means love to me

The fact that you don't say you love me
And in Actions you speak louder
And the signs showing still
Leaves me with hopes always
For that means love to me.

HAPPINESS

Happiness is not being rich
But enjoying what's within our reach
That is happiness
Living a life blameless

Happiness is not living a fancy life
With fear, pride and worry
Happiness is loving others
And sharing the little we have

Happiness is not how much we do
Happiness is the small things we do
That changes our lives
And an impact to others

Happiness is not how much we have
Or competing on how much we can give
Happiness is having nothing
But trying to make others smile with the little we have

Happiness is not being selfish
Happiness is sharing
Happiness is caring
Happiness is Love

A LETTER TO THE HEAVENS

The sky has been blue
Since ages ago
Before I was born
Or even more, conceived

The sun has been shinning
Since the start of time
Blessing as with light
Not forgetting energy

But this is too much
Our brothers are scorched
Burnt by the sun rays
Like roasted meat in feasts

Hunger is tearing them apart
Yet no one sees the burden
We are helpless perhaps
And a letter of help we write

Let me not write a long one
For the message will fade
Or perhaps, God,
You will get tired reading perhaps

But, just like in the good holy book
During the time of Moses
And those children of yours
Shower manna and quills today

We are dying of hunger
The earth has forsaken us
The rains have long deserted us
And the sun is mocking us

See, dear Lord, I haven't said much
Just asked for a little favor
To my brothers and sisters
And your reply, I'll be waiting

NIGHTFALL

Make them believe
Write to the readers,
Read to the blind
Make signs to the deaf and dumb,
Tell the young and the old too

Let them understand,
Let them know the truth,
And forget their future past
Do not cease to correct everyone,
Let them know Night is coming,

Dusk is coming
Tell them, the blame won't be yours
You won't bare the pain
Though the mountains may fall
The rivers may over flow
Or lakes and oceans dry up

Don't cease, don't halt
Don't break the pot soon
Don't let them laugh last,

Make them appreciate
And call you a hero
Let them carry sticks and twigs,
Not for a fight, no
To celebrate, to thank,

Nightfall, the sun is setting,
No moon tonight
The clouds have covered the sky black
The twinkling stars aren't twinkling like ago

But when the people hear,
And keep in mind the warning by you
They will light their own
They will bright the earth.
When dusk will be dawn
And ours will be done

WHEN I DIE

When I die, and leave the world
When I breathe my last, without a word
Don't cry, for my soul will wander
Or perhaps haunt you to the grave

When I die, don't take me to the morgue
Buy me a red casket, with black handles
And don't hire a hearse, no
Carry me in your shoulders, and don't tire

When I die, don't hire women to wail
Don't invite many visitors at my burial
Food is scarce, and I save you the trouble
Instead, bury me at night, at full moon

When I die, laugh and make merry
Celebrating the life we once lived
Eat and drink to your fill
For never will we meet

When I die, burn all my belongings
So that the memories of my life
That perhaps can bring depression
Follows me in smoke, to the land of the dead

When I die, don't whisper to each other
Stand in crowds, shout to all who care
Tell them how I cried while dying
Tell them how I choked to death

When I die, don't say I was Killed
Poisoned by love and life, No
Say I died, and you only know of my death
And not the cause of my death.

AND THAT IS WHY

I remember the calls I made
The late nights I tried to reach you
And the unanswered calls I made
Not forgetting the un replied messages

I remember the way I tried to explain myself
Yet you claimed I'm just complaining
That I do not understand at all
Yet my heart was still aching

I remember the sacrifices I made
Staying awake all night, stomach rumbling
Pretending not to be sleepy
Yet I made sure you ate Pizza

Don't ask why I left,
I just explained myself
It was too much to bare
And that is why

I loved deeply, but I loved a wrong person
I wanted attention, all I got was neglects
I wanted communication, I got silence
And that is why

Not that I didn't love at all
The problem was that I loved too much
And for granted you took my love
Like a puppet, you wanted to control me

And my emotions couldn't allow
And my heart bled a lot
And a remedy was to be found
And that is why.

A LOYAL FRIEND

She is one loyal friend
Who never betrays at all
And promises she keeps
Not to break one
Her name is death,
A unique but beautiful name
That even the strongest of all fear
But still I find myself loving her

I know one day we will meet dear
Cause I've heard of your loyalty
And your failure to betray
Dear friend, I will see you soon

I've heard of your kindness
Relieving pain for those who suffer
And I see your extra generosity
When you volunteer to take them to safety

How will I show you my love, dear death?
But to wait till we meet, and silently follow
I promise to kiss your lips
And thank you for your kindness

Dear death, wherever you are
Know that I adore you
I thank you for your generosity
Not forgetting your Kindness

Till we meet loyal Friend
For now let me count my betrayers
And those who make me sad
And later, will tell you all

ENCOUNTER WITH A LOYAL FRIEND

Yesterday she came, when the night was black
Covered by shining spots reflecting in the waters
When the earth was covered with cold
And she wanted to take me

I saw her smile, cold and sad
I smiled back, but hers was wicked
Her eyes illuminated my bed
I felt cold, then like fire, her gaze burned my soul
The urge to follow her escaped me

She was not who I supposed to be
She was cold and skinny
And wore dull black rags
And red eyes, like hot coal
And hands possessed long, formless fingers

"Come dear one," she smiled
And horror struck me
For my urge to leave had left me
And neither had I the desire
Nor the will to be friends

This Loyal one, whom I desired
Whom I longed for our meeting
Had come now, but I said no
And she was angry, and she screamed
And pangs of fire dropped from her mouth

Dear one, I know you are angry at me
But promises are to be broken
And mine promise to be a friend I break
For I've changed my mind
And I'm not coming with you.

CURSED

As dawn approached, and chirping increased
I was forced to wake up, not by will
But by the feasting of the big hungry bugs
And the pain from my ribs, as they bore the marks of my wooden
homemade pile of woods

I open the shacks of metals in place of the door
And "whoosh", am washed by the previous day's waste
Thrown aimlessly by my fat, selfish and proud neighbor
Of which some find their way through my mouth and nostrils

Angry, and in need of revenge,
I rush out of my shack, raging with fire
Fist clenched, muttering curses aloud
Neighbors rush out of their shacks
Laughing and pointing at me,
And I realized I'm clothed by God's love only

Muttering and cursing under my breathe
Half running, half walking I enter my shack
Finding that the milk I bought yesterday
By the hard earned money I got from begging
Was being feasted on by mama Toto's kittens

I raise my leg, to give them a kick
But I miss and knock out the sufuria
Which possessed the only "githeri" left for the entire week
And perhaps till mama Sam calls another plate for me
Or baba Sam calls me for supper the other week

SHADOWS OF THE MOON

Silently watching, like how owls do
Silent like the graves of the witches
Where no one wants to mention
Leave alone to tip toe and peep

Cluttering and banging,
Shingling and swashing
Wallowing and galloping
But silence remains silent

They were seen, hiding at the moon's shadow
They talked in whispers, lowered heads
In black big hoods, hiding their faces
And feared not the shadows

With knives, long pointed and ugly
Shining on the reflections of the moon
And shouting at the silence of the dark
They bored, and held hands

Under the shadows of the moon
They chanted and whispered
Laughing hysterically at times
To break the tense monotony

The shadows of the moon faded
Dark over-ruled the moon light
A scream was heard, a groan followed
Laughter echoed, breaking the silence

The moon fought back,
But the shadows were no more
The knives no more
Blood, blood flooded the earth
At the shadows of the moon

YES I DO

I still remember the kisses we kissed
Under the watch of the moon and stars
As we danced against the cold breeze
And held each other for warmth

I still remember how we fought
When I refused to take you out
I remember the day I slept at the sofa
Just because you washed our favorite sheet

I don't know, but I still remember the pain
Emotional Pain you inflicted
In my young innocent heart
And made us to part unwillingly

Yes I do, even though you made me happy
And made me have heavens on earth
You still left a hole in my heart
That until now, as I write, I feel pain

I still love you, I know,
But someone came, someone good too
She helped me recover, and still does
But the scar remains, reminding me of you

THE ME IN ME

The me that is in me is not me
The me in me is different
Not like the me I knew ago
Or the me that I wanted to be

The me in me smiles not
He cries and always moody
He complains of life going amiss
And sometimes wishes to die

The me in me has changed remarkably
Spends time alone in cemeteries
And sings songs of suicides
And laughs loud at the mention of death

The me in me
He spends time and money on drugs
Drinking until late at night
And often sleeps in ditches

The me in me needs help
I think he is depressed,
And just like others, needs help
To overcome the sorrow and heavy laden

WRITE ME A LETTER

Write me a long letter
Not of love like we used to
Not of job application letter again
But write me a letter, to remind me of the past

Write me a letter,
Reminding me of happiness
Make me remember my smiles
And the way I used to laugh until midnight

Write me a letter, and remind me of joy
Remind me the way we used to talk to noon
The way I used to make jokes
And laugh when it gets funnier

Write me a long letter
To remind me how a mentor I was
And the way I used to wipe you tears
And made you smile when you felt down

Write me a letter,
And convince me to come home
And tell me how you miss me
And the joy I inflicted in your hearts

Write me a letter,
And tell me to be sane
And stop picking food from bins
And remind me of good food at home

Write me a letter,
And urge me to stop chasing kids
And remind me the way I loved Tiffany
My little baby sister

Write me a letter,
That will change the meaning of love
And make me come home
And make me happy again

I FOUND SOLACE

I remember days ago, those doomed days
When depression was a reflection of my soul
And my eyes were painted black
And my face of wrinkled skin
And I sit down and smile,

I found solace somewhere
And I'm not selfish either, not at all
To share this mutual understanding
And the discovery of self-happiness
That won't be gotten anywhere
But from the solace within

My happiness comes from self-acceptance
Of no denial of the bitter black past
But the embracement of my old self
And learning from the bitter thorns
Of life, of love, of pain, of torture
And re-writing of the better me

I found a solace within me
And accepted that at times I'm wrong
Not worth it at all, and pain will be part of me
I found my solace
To dust off the dust in my eyes
And sweep the webs of fear and sorrow

The secret of happiness
Told by my inner self, my solace
To accept my mistakes, my pains
To forgive, to move on, and love
"Depression is a disease", He said
"And you have to choose,
Between a doctor and a patient"

DEAR FATHER'S WIFE

You are not worthy to be called a Mum
For my knowledge for you is limited
To the wife of my father
And not the mother to her children

Father said you left home,
Without a word,
And he waited till dusk
Hungry and worried

You never turned up even at dawn
Even though you knew of father's Health
Suffering from Cancer, dying
And as he cried, I could feel the pain of his tears
For what was left of him was not a man
But a corpse, waiting for death to visit

Father fought for His health
To give us hope and strength
For he toiled and sacrificed for our well being
And sometimes slept hungry to fill our small bellies
Where were you, father's wife?
When dad laid in hospital for months
When he was reduced to bones
Where were you?
When we cried for help, mmh?

And now you come,
Proudly claiming to be our mother
As if we were toys to play with
Where were you?
And now you come, to grab what is left for us.

You have filled your belly with evil money
And the wants of the world
And left us in tatters, pain and poverty
And now you want to take us
To feed us with evil money

No, dear father's wife
Let us burry father in tatters,
For that's what we lived for
Let his soul rest in piece
Not by the heavy laden of gold and silver
That you wish to buy our love with

We refuse to call you mother
For our mother is dead, inside my father's soul
We will dig two graves for him, to bare our burden
And then, we will ask for your leave
For dusk is coming, and we have to go to bed

DEAR MAMA

Mama, our teacher taught us A to Z
And Papa bought me a pen and paper
And our letter to you, papa's and mine
I write as my first test of writing

Mama, papa says that I've grown fat
But guess what! I think I could be fatter with you here
But it's a pity you aren't here, and that fills my heart with pain
And eyes to over flood with tears

Mama, even though I'm not old enough
But I am older enough to know
And understand that since you left us,
Papa and I, you will never come back
And sometimes, I find papa crying in his bedroom

Mama, this is a secret between me and you
Since you left, Papa tells me "mama do this, mama do that,"
And I smile a lot, for it reminds me when you were here
And used to tell me the same, "mama do this, mama do this"

But mama, I know papa said that you won't come back
But believe me mama, if you read this letter
And knew how People came home weeks after you left
And dug a big hole in front of our small hut
And brought a big black box, with a lady just like you inside it I believe
you will come.

Mama, at first I thought that it was you
But then I remembered that you had no white clothes,
And unlike you, the lady couldn't speak
Even when I tried to call her
Mama, I laughed as she was put in the hole
Then I saw papa cry, and until date I wonder why

Mama, I wish you were here to see
Sometimes, when papa is not around
I take a spade and hoe, and try to dig the mound
And when you come, mama
I know you will help me dig it up, and take the lady out.

Mama, papa has made me porridge
And I have to take it hot
Before doing my Homework
And later go to sleep
Mama, until you come, I will still be waiting
I love you, Papa loves you, we love you mama

THE SACRIFICES WE MAKE

You will feed us with honey and milk
To bribe us away from the pain
But the memories will be buried deep within us
Plunging deep down the thoughts of sorrow
Like a small ship lost in the middle of a raging sea
Or a plane in the middle of a stormy night
And silently, within the verge of our sorrow
We will summon death for comfort
And take pain with us
To ease the burden in our hearts

We will laugh together 'till midnight
To give you hopes of triumph
And a sense of victory and pride
But when we lay silently in our beds
In the cold lonely nights,
The buried memories will find their way out
To torment and lure us to pain
Mocking and making fun at us
As we bath in tears of our sorrows
And fighting ourselves back to slumber

Nights will not be time to sleep
For fear will be roaming at the darkest hours
Waiting to pounce on our beaten souls
And take control of the long nights
We will be enslaved by our memories
Tortured by the past bitter pains
To the point of breaking our souls
And killing the little joy we possessed
Extinguishing the light lit years ago
And hope and happiness will float in the dark

We will laugh and smile all day
And you will praise us for our happiness
And urge others to be like us
To follow the steps we ought to make
But you won't understand our grieves
And not notice the masks we wear
That fades as dusk approaches
Leaving us naked, afraid and lonely

And the chains of fear will be put on us
As we wait for our long night of torture
You won't see the sorrow behind our joy
Neither The ugly part of our beauty
Nor sense the fears behind our courage
For our masks are only worn at dawn
To give us a false impression of joy
Of courage, of happiness and of love
And you will marvel and make merry
Of how you succeeded to change us
And people will praise and sing songs for you
But we will still wait for night, for torture

ON THAT EVENING

That Evening when I picked the phone
She poured her heart out
And made my eyes flood with tears
As I listened to her confessions

She poured her heart out
Telling how her life was made in hell
And the confessions that she made
Made my heart wail in shock

Her life was made in hell
Leading her to do drugs and sell honey
And my heart wailed in shock
When she said that she had the virus

She did drugs and sold honey
To anyone ready to buy
And when she got the virus
Her life made a turn towards the pit

She sold honey to anyone ready to buy
I listened, my eyes flooding with tears
On how her life had made a turn
On that evening when I picked the phone

I WILL WAIT

I will wait until dawn
I will not let you down

When dusk falls again
I will stay not in vain

In the fields you fight
The dark will turn light

My belly is growing
I feel him kicking

Don't fail my love
You are the one I have

You are stronger than all
And I don't expect a fall

I will wait until dawn
I will not let you down

I AM A PROUD ALBINO

Neither black nor white
Somewhere in between
But I am Me,
The proud self of my version

I am just like you
Born from a woman,
With same strength and weakness
The same fears and courage

My wants of life,
Of love and equality
Strengthens my will to stand
And say I am human

I am a proud Albino
Speaking for the voiceless
Fighting for my presence
And life of acceptance

WEEDS

The farmers have deserted me
No one to take care of me now
Am branded an outcast
And weeds are growing rapidly

Farmers! Farmers! Farmers!
Where are you, I need help
Somewhere to lean on
Why let weeds choke me?

The weeds of sorrows and sadness
Are chocking the joy and happiness in me
The weeds of depression are killing me
I'm not fertile anymore, help!

You were so close to me, I remember
Until the day weeds came, and grew
And termed me infertile, you never helped
And weeds grew, I wish to die

Someone save me before am chocked to death
Before the weeds of sorrow and sadness
The weeds of silence and depression
Before I die of weeds

BY FAITH, BY HOPE

I never grew up like other children
I never knew the meaning of family
Mama, died at my birth
And Papa left the same noon

My only home was at the streets
Taken care by older street children
And one Maria made me her child
A street mama's child

I knew not of joy and happiness
For my little joy was destroyed
By the older rough street brothers
And was forced to beg for them

It's by faith and hope
Patience and perseverance
That I took all the blows and abuses
That I waited for my stars to re appear

Maria died when I was five
Leaving me with bullies, in total five
Who beat me every morning?
And abused me if I was found crying

I still don't understand how,
But during the floods of the late 90's
That swept my home and world
Made my life light blue

Mama Natasha, my foster mama
Took me by my hands
Cold bitten and beaten by rains
Washed and made me hers.

WRITE ME A LETTER

Write me a long letter
Not of love like we used to
Not of job application letter again
But write me a letter, to remind me of the past

Write me a letter,
Reminding me of happiness
Make me remember my smiles
And the way I used to laugh until midnight

Write me a letter, and remind me of joy
Remind me the way we used to talk to noon
The way I used to make jokes
And laugh when it gets funnier

Write me a long letter
To remind me how a mentor I was
And the way I used to wipe you tears
And made you smile when you felt down

Write me a letter,
And convince me to come home
And tell me how you miss me
And the joy I inflicted in your hearts

Write me a letter,
And tell me to be sane
And stop picking food from bins
And remind me of good food at home

Write me a letter,
And urge me to stop chasing kids
And remind me the way I loved Tiffany
My little baby sister

Write me a letter,
That will change the meaning of love
And make me come home
And make me happy again

BEFORE YOU SAY 'I DO'

This is the most beautiful night
Swimming in the midst of the stars
But my heart is beating hard
Anticipating for what comes after this

I want you to marry me,
And become the mother to my babies
But before you say "I Do"
I have many things to confess

I want to understand what I say
I am not ashamed of my home at all
But will you bare a one meal per day?
That is all my family can afford

Will you stay with me forever?
Even when I say I am poor
And cannot afford a multi-billion wedding
The dream wedding you told me about

Before you say "I Do"
I want you to know for sure
What life I've lived for long
And where I came from

Don't make your mind in a hurry
And If possible, take your time to think
And if you say No to my proposal
Be sure I will understand the reason why

SUN-DAY OR SUNDAY?

I don't know how to explain this
I know for sure I will be criticized
And perhaps many will call me a pagan
Or a hypocrite to make the matters worse

But it's itching; I just want to say it
I'm not a Pagan I know, neither a hypocrite
But what my eyes have seen in churches
Is enough for me to stay at home on Sundays

The other Sunday I was late for church
At 12 pm I found myself at the back of the church
Full of believers and saints
And the ushers came to me,
With empty baskets of offerings

I could have given them All I had I swear
But then the pastor began preaching
And told me how God will bless me today
In conditions I couldn't understand
Yet he began naming them one by one

Hallelujah, the pastor shouted
If you want God to bless you today
And by tomorrow be rich with silver and gold
Be full with honey and milk
He wiped sweat from his face

Deep your hands in your pockets
And not less than a thousand shillings not
Drain your pockets in the basket
And the church ululated with happiness
And the front benchers waved notes in the air

I looked at a woman besides me
Old, in tatters and dirt
She held a silver coin, one shilling to be precise
Looked at it for a second
Before dipping it into her dirty pockets
Before the ushers escorted her to the exit

The ushers who came to me earlier
Looked at the woman with disgust
Turned back at me
Looked at the empty basket, looked back at me
Before their soft hands pointed at the exit
And I was too wise to question

THE GIFT OF FRIENDSHIP

It's the second day of the month
And how I wish I could write earlier
To wish you the best in this month
And the months to follow this

I wish I could have written earlier
But my mind was full of praises
And I wondered what to write
And what to leave out in my writing

I will try to write what is best
To thank you for the gift of love
And the bond we share since long ago
Of friendship, of togetherness, of love

My memories take me back to where it all started
Two strangers who met,
I believe that fate played its part
To see you and I journey together

I won't forget how you held my back
Even when the world turned against me
Like a shadow you followed still
And whispered your whispers of courage

I owe you my flesh and life
Even when it hurt, you still persevered
You were rained on to give me shelter
Scorched by the sun to make me a shade

You are priceless, not even gold can buy you
And of all the gifts I may think of
I settle for my friendship to you
And with it, I carry loyalty

SHOULD I?

It's amazing how the world is
And today, I meet two new strangers
And you still argue with me
Claiming to be papa and mama

Ha-ha, it's funny to hear you speak
And you tears, whether of joy or sorrow
Is not enough to convince me
Of the tales you keep telling me

Fifteen years down the line
And I wonder if you tossed in your beds
Did you even dream of me at times?
And like other parents, try to find me?

My papa and mama, all I know
Are those who toss filthy coins
On their way down the streets
To homes and places of work

For fifteen years I've lived
Spend time with the only family I had
The filthy thin dogs
And the dirty ever hungry pigs

From the blue sky you fall
To ask for my forgiveness
And how you missed me
And never slept since fifteen years ago

I find it amusing,
And if you don't mind
I have to scavenge for food
Before my family finds the best for themselves.

Should I?
Should I call you papa and mama?
No, my papa will toss me a coin
My mama will leave a crumb of bread at her doorstep

For fifteen years I've lived
The cobblers glue gave me comfort
My family, the dogs and filthy dirty pigs
Never made me feel lonely

Should I?
Should I call you papa?
Should I call you mama?
Tell me, Should I?

REBECCA

Rebecca, oh Rebecca, Rebecca
When you pass by my home, Rebecca
On your way to the river, Rebecca
Please try to whistle, Rebecca
Or sometimes call my name.

When you see me standing by the road
Do not shy away, Rebecca
My heart yearns to speak, speak to you Rebecca
And even when the sun sets, Rebecca
I always stand by the road, watching you pass by

Rebecca, My eyes watch you sway hips
My mouth gapes, as you take each step
Mama, Rebecca, should I remind you
Rebecca, that it is love, not illusions?
I'm growing older, and, Rebecca,
I want you as a wife, you Rebecca

Rebecca, I am not a coward, they say
I fought the War of the Whites,
Rebecca, as the song of the poets goes
With a spear on hand, Rebecca,
I, myself, chopped the white man's head
Of these tales, I am not bragging, Rebecca

Rebecca, when you pass by my home
Please knock and say hello
Rebecca, my hands are tired of fighting
My hands yearn to touch the soft skin
Rebecca, not anyone's, your skin Rebecca

Rebecca, pass by home tomorrow
Color my walls with your beauty
Light my hut with your smile, Rebecca
Come Rebecca, See, I am strong and handsome
Hardworking and brave
Rebecca, a suitable husband for a suitable wife

Rebecca, oh Rebecca, Rebecca
The moon of the village,
Rebecca, the one with stars in the eyes
Who will marry you Rebecca?
Tell me, if you don't stop by my home
And say hello, Rebecca, oh Rebecca.

ARE WE STILL IN LOVE?

I was sitting alone today,
Just outside the fence
Contemplating on days ago
When our love was full of life

Those late night calls
The jokes and plays in the evenings
The late night talks and calls
Are fading, like dawn to dusk

You loved me, days ago,
But today, I see the shadows of love
The love you gave days ago
When we were young in love

Our love has changed of late
From actions to words
From late night calls, to weeks without talks
And I keep wondering still

Are we still in love?
Or the illusions are fading
Like colors off walls
Do we still have that love?

IF YOU MEET ME

I don't know how to explain this
It may be hard for me to explain
I bet you won't believe too
But I'm lost, and I need help

If you meet me on that path
That path I chose to lead
Call me by name
And hold me if you can

If you see me tonight
When dusk turns black
Come closer to me
And bring with you a candle

Remind me my name
Remind me my purpose
Beg me to follow your path
And persist if I refuse

If you see me in chains
Don't turn your back on me
I am just but a slave
Who needs to be freed

So, if you meet me
If you see me by chance
Call me by my name
Hold me if you can

WHERE I COME FROM, WHERE I CALL HOME

This place that I call home
This humble place with humble people
The place my ancestors lived
My grandparents grew
My parents were born
The place I call home

The pride of our homeland
The pride of our blood, our culture
These that never cease to amaze me
The isikuti dances, the isikuti dancers
The way they shake their shoulders
You my fear they may break

The obusuma and ingoho
Aha! The pride of our food
That which represent our culture
That which makes us be the Abaluyha
Ingoho, say no more, Obhusuma
Our food, our culture

I come from the Abaluyha
The people from western Kenya
Those who dance the mulongo dance
The songs of the young men
The beautiful songs of initiation
The pride of our culture
The pride of our men

Have you ever seen bull fights?
The place I call home, the place I come from
We have bull fights, bull fighting is our pride
From far and wide we converge
We sing and dance
Eat and drink, haa, the liquor we call busaa
Our pride, our culture.

Nafula and Wafula our pride
Nekesa and Wekesa our people
The Abaluyha we are
The men and women of Ingoho
We are the Obusuma people
And we are amazing
The place I come from, the place I call home.

I PLEAD NOT GUILTY

When my phone rang that night
I couldn't hear it ringing
And she was within reach
Just like other days before
She took the call again

I was at the bathroom, I remember
And she sat at the coach
Listening to the caller
And she never said a word
But the tears in her eyes, spoke the words

The "secretary" had called
And she answered the call
"I am carrying your child"
She heard her echo the words
"And I want to share a home with you"

The food she cooked stayed cold
The bed she warmed stayed cold
That night she looked at me
Tears of hurt and betrayal
She saw the lie in me

I pledge not guilty
For the story was long
And only if she gives time
And promises to listen
I will tell her about her

I pledge not guilty
And I will send a messenger tomorrow
To tell her to come home
To cook the sweetest food
To warm our cold bed
And listen to the true story

WHY NOW?

When the rain was raining
You came to me for shade
I gave you my warmth
Not forgetting my whole heart
Until the rain stopped, then you left

You claim to love me,
Yet, without goodbye you left
You despised me after all I did
The sacrifice I made, that led to nothing
Yet you say you love me

Isn't she giving you the love you needed?
Remember the tears I shed
When you, you left without a word
The words you threw to me
How much you love her, you claimed
And never wanted us to be together

For a year you claimed you loved me
And the promises were for you to be mine
Which indeed you broke without a thought
And when the sun rose, you left
Torn my heart into pieces
That I'm still looking for other pieces

I am not boarding
I am not listening to lies
I am not taking the promises
My wounds are healed not
And In love, I do not believe
Why Now?

BLACK HEART

Love, they say is happiness
Love, they say is life
But mine is not happiness
Mine is not life, Love

But mine is not happiness
That grew from the roots
With flowers that bloom
No, it's a reflection of love
That carries with it sadness

If only she knew my heart
And stop saying she loves
But look into mine eyes
The black part of my heart
And wash me clean

She says that she loves me
Yes, I don't doubt at all, do I?
But perhaps the black heart
Painted white with love
Is fading to black, dirty black

I want to die and leave
For my love is black with dark
Smelling rotten eggs
Lost in the abyss of darkness
With no holds and touches

I want someone to make her happy
One with clean white heart
Not black, or painted one, like mine
No, this is a wish of a dying heart
Before my eyes are closed tomorrow

Tomorrow, I will die
But let her celebrate my black death
Let her believe I was black and bad
For I hear death calling
And who I'm I to decline?

DREAMS OF MY FATHER

My father's dream was to make me a man
Not only a man, but a better man
A better strong man
A strong and courageous man
Dreams of my father

My father's dream was to make me wise
Not only wise, but a wise man
A wise educated man
An educated and smart man
Dreams of my father

 My father's dream was to make me rich
Not only rich, but a kind rich man
A kind and generous rich man
Generous and humble rich man
Dreams of my father.

My father's dream was to make me happy
Not only happy, but a healthy man
A healthy and wealthy man
Wealthy and a joyful man
Dreams of my father.

THE THINGS YOU LIED TO ME

You lied to me
You promised to die with me
You promised to die for me
But remember Last year,
When the car accident killed me
And am still waiting here,
For your death
For you to die
For us to journey together
Tell me, for how long should I wait?

Even before I died, when we were together
You promised not to leave my side
You said I am the world to you
I still remember,
But what hurts more
Is the fact that you never stepped at the morgue
You were afraid even to look at my scars
And I heard that you never attended my burial

I am not complaining at all
But just reminding you of the broken promises
I love you even in my death
And my heart bleeds all through
When I remember the lie we lived
And my death has proven me right

Expectations are wrong, see
I expected you to die
I waited for a year for your death
The pain of waiting between death and life
The storm that I persevered
To wait for you, the one I love
But I heard you were happy
And had no intention of dying

You are a lie
We lived a lie
And as I journey to the land of the dead
I leave my broken heart to wait for you
I leave my soul and memories
To remind you of the things you lied
To reflect the reflections of your lie
Love is a lie, and death always confirm that

BROKEN POTS

The days that equality was a song
Understanding was the lyrics
And love and peace were the drums
The days are long gone, gone

We are left to suffer the inequalities
To face the misunderstandings
To mend the broken pieces
Like stray dogs in the market

We are forced to swallow our tears
To keep to the inner self
For fear of discovery, discrimination
And we kill our soul, our self

Broken pots, cowards
Who can't hold a drop of water
Too broken to carry the weight
Broken pots, yes we are

Fear to mend ourselves
Like crying babies at a nursery
Too weak to help themselves
Crying for help, help not coming

We are broken, broken pots
We are dying, dying souls
Cowards, fear to face challenges
Broken Pots, Broken Pieces

ROSES ARE RED

Blooming with flowers
Purple and blue flowers
Tall and short flowers
Not roses, Roses are red

Roses are red
Like old wine
Like oozing blood
Bright Red Roses

They shine like morning sun
A reflection on the dew
Or broken mirrors reflected
Like diamonds on the ground

Like old wine
Like fresh blood
Red roses bloom
Roses, Red roses

Air filled with fragrance
Air filled with birds
Nectar sucking birds
Perching on red roses

Roses are red
Red like red
Blood and wine
Roses are blooming

MAMA'S VOICES

Hush, little baby, hush my child
Milk is in plenty
Food is in abundance

    Cry no more
    Mama knows your needs
    Hush baby, hush my child

The rain will bring flowers
The fragrances will fill the air
And mama will pluck a rose for you

    Mama loves you baby
        Mama cares

Hush little baby, hush my child
Papa will come tomorrow
And together we'll take a walk

TOMORROW AT MY BURIAL

So tomorrow my eulogy will be read
And many will wonder
Beneath the smiles and happiness
Scars that never healed will be seen

Those who seemed to care
Will be shocked to be named the cause
Not only of my death but suffering
And all will wail

The sacrifices I made
Will be read to all
And many will be filled with guilt
And wished they knew

But I will be dead
And my body will smell of rot
And my eyes will pop out
To torment their souls

Tomorrow, at my burial
Chaos will be faced
Sadness will cover them all
Like a big black blanket.

THE WOMAN IN MY DREAMS

I know you all know her,
The woman in my dreams
For it is not a secret anymore
But a mirror of my dreams
To reflect what I dream of all night

I met her years ago,
When our bloods were boiling
In search of love and affection
But distance threatened ours love
Until the day we fought over it all

She was stubborn as ever
Not interested in love from a boy
A boy she's never seen before
And not willing to give her heart out
But like a parasite still stayed unshaken

Her love was hidden somewhere within
And it took days of persistently asking
And nights of calling and texting
Till she came into terms
And uncovered the precious hidden love

She has stayed for as long as I can count
And I see no sign of her leaving
For like a big rock under the ocean
She is strong and patient
The woman in my dreams

I LIED

Do you remember our first date?
When I took you out for dinner
And we danced the whole night
Do you remember?

I told you many lies ever since
And I'm not at peace until I confess
And my hopes are for you to understand
That was the past, and I changed

You were my first lover, was a lie
You were my first kisser, was a lie
I've never cheated on you, was a lie
I love you with all my heart, was a lie

I lied; I lied so that I can win you
I lied; I lied to prove them wrong
My friends,
I lied; I lied to have fun with you

AFRICA, MY PRIDE, MY SOIL

I am the child of the soil, a patriot
Under the umbrella of mama Africa
Adorable and caring, mama Africa
I am a product of her beauty
And her diverse knowledge and wisdom

Africa, my pride, my soil
From the cultures across the continent
Rich culture, from generation to the next
That carries the mark of our communities
The pride and sense of belonging
From the north to the south

Did I forget about you beauty, mama?
The beauty of nature you carry
The long rivers and the high mountains
The deep valleys and the wide lakes
The thick, green trees
That builds our indigenous forests

Mama Africa, your love for wildlife
From the wild beasts in Kenya and Tanzania
The rare animals in the heart of your body
These attractions like magnets
Your way of attracting visitors
Mama Africa, who I'm I to deny your love?

Mama Africa, once again, I remember
The folksongs you taught us
That praises our culture, diverse culture
The stories given to us, by our ancestors
That which we cling on, that which we pass through
Mama, our rich traditions, our knowledge

Who I'm I not to be called the son of the soil?
Who I'm I to deny you Mama Africa?
You are rich, you made us rich
The mines, the gold and diamonds
Precious gift,
The ornaments, the soil and beauty
The rains and fertile lands
These are enough gifts Mama.

Mama Africa, My pride, my land
I am a proud son of the Land
Mama Africa has proven to be rich
Mama Africa has proven to be wise
The memories she keeps

ARE WE STILL IN LOVE?

I was sitting alone today,
Just outside the fence
Contemplating on days ago
When our love was full of life

Those late night calls
The jokes and plays in the evenings
The late night talks and calls
Are fading, like dawn to dusk

You loved me, days ago,
But today, I see the shadows of love
The love you gave days ago
When we were young in love

Our love has changed of late
From actions to words
From late night calls, to weeks without talks
And I keep wondering still

Are we still in love?
Or the illusions are fading
Like colors off walls
Do we still have that love?

WHAT IS LOVE?

Tell me what love is,
Is it that feeling of attraction between two people?
Or just having lustful feelings,
Is it just a word?

That people play around with,
Is it just a game?
With sex as a goal,
I thought love is that feeling,

Of being comfortable in ones presence,
Having your best moments in ones silence,
A sense of belonging in ones life,
Emptiness when missing someone,

I wish in love,
I will breathe in peace, and cast the pain away,
I will heal my brokenness and feel myself whole,
I will not be afraid of getting hurt again,

I will have a voice and not only follow orders,
Hope to love and be loved back,
That true love from an honest person,
I wish to know what love is

JUST BECAUSE I AM A GIRL

Just because I am a girl,
They want me to stay at home.
Or worst still to 'cook' for someone
Someone older and wealthier
Someone with money, cows and wives
Someone with children, grand children and great grand children
Just because I am a girl

Just because I am a girl
They take me out of the keys of life
Forcing me to cook, wash and collect firewood
They sit and laugh loud
As I coil, bitten by smoke and soot
Coughing and battling with smoke
In the dark pits full of utensils

Just because I am girl
They snatch me freedom of speech
To listen and agree to their judgments
To argue not even when I am right
They make bad decisions on my behalf
And like a lamb supposed to follow still
Just because

Just because I am a girl
I am forced to be mutilated
Cut by the ugly blunt old iron
To scream not for help
But behave like a well taught woman
To carry countless children in my small belly
Children who know not their fate
And cursed and shunned away if I get no 'men'

Just because I am a girl
Does not mean I can't be educated
Just because I am a girl
Does not mean I can't speak
Just because

Just because I am a girl
Does not mean I am no human
I am a girl
And a human for that matter
My rights I will fight for
I am tired of 'cooking'
Tired of marrying my grandfathers
I am tired of being cut
And the pain is painful
Just because I am a girl

MY CALENDAR READS 17

Today I took a pen and paper
And changed the theme of my letter
Not those I send on tenth
For they were colored in black
And wet with tears

I stopped loving years ago,
Not that I am human not
No, Maria left me, without a word
And made my world black
With patches or red and white

But today, seventeen on the calendar
I open my heart to Natalia
And accept the offer to be happy
To love again, to taste her love
And forget Maria's Memories

So, when you read this letter
Erase the data of the previous one
And rewrite my name again
On your old book of love
For Natalia has light, my light

TAX COLLECTORS

Ding dong, goes the bell
The door opens wide
They Rush in and out
Like busy bees on errands

They flood the gates
With big round bellies
Like big ripe pumpkins
Collecting notes and cents

They stink of filth
Flies for followers
Buzzing hymns of hunger
To devour the cents collected

Tax collectors,
Collecting taxes from husbands
And sometimes leave change
Seen nine months later

Ding Dong, goes the bell
They flood in the open bars
Carrying empty hungry bellies
Later filled with taxed booze

A KIND SOUL

A kind soul is not being rich,
But enjoying what's within reach.
That is a kind soul
Living a life blameless

A kind soul is not living a fancy life
With fear, pride and worry
A kind soul is loving others
And sharing the little we have

Kindness is not how much we do
Kindness is the small things we do
That changes our lives
And an impact to others

Kindness is not how much we have
Or competing on how much we can give
Kindness is having nothing
But trying to make others smile with the little we have

BLOOD AND ASH

We live in fear of fellow neighbors
Our enemies are those we trusted
We hate those we loved, ages ago
Our hearts are hurt and rage with fire
Revenge echoes, louder, gaining courage

The desire to drink blood,
To subtract one, two, three, countless
To take away hearts, to chop off heads
Our bloods are getting colder, eyes popping
Hands ready to strike, death seems cheap

The fires ready to be lit
To blow brains, burn houses and cars
From filthy, unremorseful peeps
Hunger for blood and ashes
Death calls from the silent noises

It's blood and ashes, that leaves many orphans
Countless widows and widowers
Crippled, blind and paralyzed
Blood and ashes, the songs of the dead
Ringing through the echoes of hatred

Brothers turn into sisters,
Forcing themselves into forbidden gates
What a calamity, abomination, a big taboo
Men are slaughtered, like chickens in feasts
Blood flows, like the great Nile

The raging fires are eating up everything
Laughing mockingly, like baby hyenas
Our hearts turn black, with smoke
Smoke that chokes us, blocking our view
We are killing each other, dancing at the songs of the dead

The blood not shed, the ashes not burnt
The fights not fought, sisters not defiled
Not that we see, not the peace we enjoy
The fights are from within, fights in our minds
Hidden corruption, hidden tribalism
Blood and Ashes.

TILL MARRIAGE DO US PART

I'm sending you to the world
And be sure to pass my word
To any lady, or woman if any
Only one, not two or many

Send my word of courtship
To anyone ready to take terms
I want a special relationship
Like that of farmers with farms

I want to have a lover
One who will sign my contract
She who will give me her love
Till marriage do us part

I want someone to kiss
Someone to give all my love
A woman to miss
And make mine heart not to starve

Till marriage do us part
When I find a wife suitable
That my life will start
And leave without trouble

If you find one with qualities
Tell her to come for a start
We travel to all cities
Till marriage do is part

GLOWING CANDLE

Hold me tight, nightfall is coming,
The broken pieces of the broken mirrors will be mended
The dying leaves of the olive
Will rise and live once again

Don't loosen your grip
The stars won't shine,
The moon, hidden under the mercies of the angry black clouds, won't
shine
And death will fear, your grip

You will glow, like the glowing Candle
Red with love and life
Illuminating deep on the black
Warming the colds and deepest dark

LETTERS OF LOVE

I was afraid to write letters of love
Letters that knew not their fates
Torn into pieces, tattered and scrambled
Letters burnt into ashes, letters denied

Pens bled inks of sorrow
Leaving their bloody marks on some papers
Sometimes filling letters with dirt
Or making them overflow with sticky inks

Letters of love, letters not written
That stayed in minds for ages
Afraid of losing dignities and pride
Letters that could be seen flying in air

Letters of love that never escaped
Escaped the sender's grip,
Letters written with perfection
The perfect timing for love, letters.

HAPPY BIRTHDAY MAMA

I hear the birds singing,
I hear the birds flapping
Did you hear the insects too?
I hear them chirping

Mama's day is here
No wonder the sun is smiling
And yester night, I heard the moon speak
Talking to her husband, the sun
To prepare for the queen's coming

Happy birthday to you
One who held me through the storm
Gave me warmth in Ice
Gave me water in the desert
Mama, my hero, my protector

I got three flowers for you,
One, for your bravery and strength
The second is for your love and care
Mama, the third, and the last,
Is for your birthday, your born day

My queen, mama, daddy's favorite
With joy and happiness, I write
Happy birthday, happy born day
I got the biggest cake ever
Encrypted with love "I Love You Mama"

BLOOD STAINED

Like it was never enough
Even with the ear piercing screams
The blade ignored the screams
With closed ears, continued to work
Cutting and spilling blood everywhere

She was only sixteen
And the blood she shaded
The blood that filled the ocean
Changed her life completely
And made her a "woman"
Ready to be exchanged for cows

Blood stained, she cried her voice out
The scar was not only left in her body
But also her heart, her young heart
The betrayal, culture had betrayed her
Robbed her of her choices
Took the freedom of decisions away

The women ululating at the other side
Not caring the pain and agony she passed through
Competed with her screams and wails
"COWARD" they spat
"And woe befall to those who cry by the blade"
The painful, rusty and ugly blade
The ugly blade, cutting through her flesh

Blood stained, weak, hungry and angry
Pain with no gain, she suffered
Her childhood was being shattered
Her innocence revealed, unwillingly
Blood stained, she lay on the dirty dirt
Blood stained.

WHERE ARE YOU NOW?

It used to hurt you,
But like a brother, stayed silent
You wore fake smiles, to make us happy
But you were hurt, your heart was hurting
But, where are you now?

You used to praise us
And wished us a happy relationship
Talked of the beauty of our love
And the way your pride on us is unending
And ours happiness is yours happiness
But, where are you now?

You used to stay late nights with her
Laughing and making jokes
I went to bed early, always
Not worrying about you and her
Were you not my brother?
But, where are you now?

I was a fool to believe so
Blood is thicker than water, a simple lie
Like a parasite you fed on our happiness
Flirted with her, the whole night
As I lay in bed, worrying not
But where are you now?

You left, for work you claimed
A month later she left, for work she claimed
Yet, happily I bid you goodbye
With love, I let her go, for work
But where are you now?
Married, married to her, my wife.

You planned it all
And made me lose the game
She said goodbye to me
But never did I know
Our love had reached a waterfall
And like a pool of water
You waited below, patiently.

THORNS OF A ROSE part 1

Luck was not on my side,
And that was what I thought at first
As I walked down the galleys
Beaten by the heavy downpour
And my clothes soaked wet

Even when I met her at the corner
I didn't realize at first,
And thought of a giant black bull dog
And my blood froze in my veins
And transfixed to the ground, I went silent

She sat there alone
Shivering, crying and wet
And when I stood at my spot
She looked up, scared, with red eyes
That glittered at the fading half moon's reflection

Maria was her name
A beautiful name, sweet like a rose
And she hid her pains and horror behind her faint smile
And I couldn't help but smile back at her
It was midnight, 0023 to be precise

THORNS OF A ROSE part 2

I sat beside Maria,
How I did it, until now I don't know
And the waters from the sky hit us harder
But we sat, Maria and me.

Maria had this reflection on her face
That made one believe to have seen an angel
And I was no exception
But to Marvel at her beauty

"Megan," her voice fought through the rains
And echoed, like a cooing dove in my ear
And my mouth failed to utter words
For fear of provoking an angel
Or perhaps of making her stop smiling

Maria urged me to leaver her
She feared for my health,
For the cold made me shiver
And I yearned for my warm bed
Or perhaps a cuddle from her

Like a Good Samaritan, not out of lust
I begged Maria to let me take her home
For midnight was a den of evil
And I feared for her life and health
And I swore to help her out

Maria couldn't hold it more
And I heard her sniffing loudly
And I could just guess one thing
The worst that I feared and it broke my heart
She was crying.

I stood up, took her by my hands
And slowly, zigzagging through the muddy path
And sometimes getting up from our falls
I made up my mind
And had to take her home, my house
Until dawn comes, and rain seizes.

ONE DAY

One day I will take a pen and paper
One day I will know how to read and write
One day, I will re arrange the words in my mind
And change them from senseless to sense
One day

One day I will write what is right
With a permanent blue ink, to a clear white paper
One day I will write my mind out
Not complaining, not arguing, not shouting
I will write something right

One day I will look at the world in a different way
When I write what will change all
Words that will make them believe
Words to give hope, and happiness

One day I will write smiles on people's faces
I will paint on people's hearts
Writings that will over write the sorrow in them
Writings that will erase the faded doubts
And make them believe in themselves

Give me the strength to learn
The courage to explore more
And when time comes to write
I will keep you in my words
And store your courage and strength
In the writings that will change the world.

WHAT WILL YOU DO?

What will you do?
I ask myself every morning
Before even taking my phone
Or changing my pajamas
When you find a man beating a woman

If someone sees a woman beaten
And walks away as if nothing really happened
Or takes a camera and records to the last
What will you do?
To the beater and the camera man, mmh?

At times you may be walking alone
Or maybe with a group of friends
Or still with your new girlfriend
And you see a man beating a woman
What will be your first action?

I repeat what if the man beats your woman
Or perhaps, someone close to you
Will you stand still and silent?
Or will you find a way to help?
Someone answer this, someone.

Lewis Wamwanda and Chrismoh Maobe present to you:

SILENT NOISES

Behind her joy and happiness
Under her smiling face
Hidden in the back of her soul
Black, void and emptiness
She fights her silent noises

The noises that haunt
At midnight when the night is silent
When the spirits are sound asleep
When the waters are cold and still
She's up to listen to the noises from unseen faces

She sits still, in the darkness
Looks dumb and deaf
Stares at space
Gazes, lost in time
But the silent noises torture her mind

The noises sound creepy
Hard to tell what message they have
She cries to the moon and wishes for death
Counts the stars hoping they'd help
Making wishes to the fireflies and hopes death will strike before dawn
The noises are unheard but they scream in her head

She is dying, silently
She is ashamed to call for help
Afraid to silence the silent noises
She cries, depressed and sad
She, a broken vessel
She cries

She's fading
Her spirit is gone
The noises summoned her
Living under depression
She's ready to leave
Her second home waits
Tired of faking smiles
She's tormented...

Lewis Wamwanda and Chrimoh Maobe write A LETTER TO DAD
check it out:

DEAR DAD

Dear dad,
A thousand secrets to whisper to you
A million letters I want to write to you
Endless love I want to express
But how will I get you?
The title "dad" makes me shed a tear .....
I love the invisible you and miss the physical you

Dad, but still I grief your leave
I got stories to tell too
And I hope you are willing to listen
For my pen may run dry
Or my paper out of stock
But still, I have to let you know

This is my letter to you
Hope it gets you well but promise me you'll not cry when you unfold it
I don't know where you are now but I know you're there
In the clouds, in heaven or behind me...
Hope you'll read this letter....
When you left...........

When you left, papa
Mama cried for weeks,
Never ate for days, and led us to suffer
Mama brought a man home
We called him "papa"
But dad, I call him "Mama's husband"
I swear

Cause to mama, she was a husband
But never a dad to us
You are the "papa", we know
Never knew mama was so selfish
To look for a husband for herself but not a father for us
"Papa", when you left,
Our world turned upside down
We cried when you were lowered

But since "mama's husband" moved in
We've been mourning
Crying under the sheets and
Smiling in the presence of him
To avoid the whip when we say "we miss our dad"
He claims to pay my fees,
But is that enough? Dad didn't you pay fees?
You did, but fathered us
Pampered us like little angels, papa
If you read this letter
Sooner or even later
Come back to us, papa
For our lives is hell
A living hell on earth

Once again, Chrismoh Maobe and Lewis Wamwanda brings to you
UNDELIVERED LETTERS

UNDELIVERED LETTERS

Letters that we wrote
Those long letters that we wrote
Letters that dried our inks
And stopped our pens from bleeding
Letters undelivered

Our only remaining hope
Letters to bring them back to us
Those letters worth our time
Letters to our beloved
Lost into unknown world

Letters to show our love
Letters to bare out grieves
Letters to bring memories
Memories threatening to fade
The letters we wrote

Letters that made us shed tears
Letters that withdrew the blade
Hoping they'd read and come to us
Letters undelivered

Letters, posted on their graves
Letters buried with the dead
Letters that were opened not.
The letters not delivered

MY MAASAI BEAUTY

She is a Maasai lady, a beauty
She, who makes my mind go blue
And sometime my eyes turn red
Red, for lack of sleep, thinking of her

Have you seen her, perhaps no
But my Maasai lady, is a beauty
Her eyes, twinkling like morning stars
That brightens my dark skin
And gives me a sense of belonging

My Maasai lady, a gem, valuable and priceless
She is a reflection of the moon
Competing for love and affection
A symbol of love and truth.

She is clothed in smiles
That covers her face,
That which makes her Cinderella
The lucky girl in the fairy tales

HAPPY BIRTHDAY

Your smiles, your eyes, your lips
Your baby face, jovial and full of love
Molded years ago, when the sun shone
Stars twinkled and the moon smiled
Happy Birthday.

I was not there, but the stories spread
That when you, a princess was born
The winds sang, the trees danced
And the insects and birds, of all kinds
Travelled from far, to Marvell at your beauty

Happy birthday Princess
Many talked of your beauty
And the reflections of your smiles
That left many see with their mouths wide open
And not until I saw it, I had you that I believed

Many years we've lived
But still your beauty increases
As you cut cakes and open champagne
As you blow candles and pop popcorns
I, I write you a wish, to color your day

Happy Birthday,
Let my words sink into your veins
Let me color your day with joy and happiness
Let me sing songs of a new day
Happy birthday Princess.

MAMA, THANK YOU

Forty Nine is a magic number
Even before I was born
Your service to the nation was given
And After I was born, years later
Your service never ceased

Mama, it is with great pleasure
With tears of joy and happiness
Once again I take my pens and paper
To write my thoughts, and praises
Mama, thank you.

The steps that you left behind for me
The torch that you lit in the dark
For my small footsteps to step on
For my little eyes to see
Mama, how will I praise you?

The end of the journey is part of the journey
The services you served,
That changed not only my mind, but vision too
The pens you penned down
Will forever be written in our hearts

Mama, you were, and still, you are a mentor
Celebrations,
I will summon the moon and the stars
To marvel and celebrate you
Mama, flowers are blooming

I DIE TOMORROW

If I die, don't ask why,
For life has taught me lessons
And death is my exam
Let me sleep, let me die

If I die, then blame your soul
I yearned for talks, I was shunned away
I begged for love, I was given hatred
I die tomorrow, and the guilt is yours

If I die, don't cry or weep
Don't say sorry to my corpse
My soul will float
In the abyss of life and death

I die tomorrow
Tomorrow, like other days
The memories will linger
But my soul will leave

LIFE MOCKED ME YESTERDAY

Life mocked me yesterday,
And there is nothing I could do
But to wipe the tears in my eyes
And walk away, ashamed and angry

I went to the government offices
And all the soldiers could say to me
Was "move" yet the president was serving
Serving not the nation but serving his needs
And I bet the bed he slept on creaked with shame

Sad and frustrated, I walked away
To find my solace in the town church
Where God is claimed to be, at the altars
But all I could get from Priests was
"Bring not less than ten dollars as an offering"
Yet I had come for my financial wants

Yesterday life played chess with me
And I am ashamed to say I lost
My financial Wants took me to my girlfriend's
And I stood there knocking, after months
She opened the door, holding a baby on her hands
And a five feet Man behind her
And I had to ask for a cup of water, before taking my leave.

Yesterday Life mocked me,
Like a game of chess I lost
The Government was "serving the nation"
The church was "ripping believer's money"
And my girlfriend was happily married.
Yesterday, Life gave me a checkmate.

DON'T TELL HER

If you manage to go home
If your sentence elapses
If your time comes
And you leave for home
Say hello to my wife
And buy sweets for my children

If you arrive safely
Pass my greetings to my son
Say hello to my daughter
But don't tell their mother
Don't make her worried
Until I come, don't tell her yet

Don't tell her, that I have no work
That I am not even a manager
Tell her, I am on my way
Working on a bigger company
Saving for a better life
For me and for her

Don't tell her I remarried
And got a con woman,
Who wiped my pockets dry
And left me with a kid
Who later died of malnutrition
My last baby boy.

Don't tell her that I killed my boss
For he paid me peanuts
And I rented his wife
And later her daughter for a month
Before the blue men came
With guns and arms

Don't tell her, not yet
How the blue men escorted me
Like a president to his home
Made of bars and ticks

Don't tell her yet
That I am living for my crimes
Till my time elapses
Till my leave comes
Don't tell her,
I will come home soon
And tell her my tales
That will change us forever.

I SAW A BLACK MOON

From the west
A black moon, with red eyes
And trickling of fresh blood
It rose.

Fierce and raging with anger
Lust and urge to devour
Angry and hungry for blood
It cried with rage

I saw a black moon
It was flashing, lightening
Roaring, like thunder
And the blood rained from its face

It carried the sun with it
Like a young mother, with a child
It squeezed the sun's rays
Blocking them from view

I saw a black moon
A moon so black and dark
Lonely and sad
As it rained blood on my face

I AM

I Write what I am
My art can fill the heart
Like quenching thirst
In a dry hot dessert

I am what I write
For my pens are my thoughts
My words are my soul
Inking them into lines

I am a writer, a poet
Lines that flow
Trickling on a steep cliff
Seeps through the vein

I am a poem
With letters and words
Bringing the death to life
Shaping the words to lines

See, I am, who I am
I am a writer
I am a poet
I am.

WE ARE JUST FRIENDS

Do you remember those days?
When we talked till nightfall
When we laughed till dawn
Till she came, and made a difference

You were mad at me
Accused me of loving too much
I heard your voice, of anger
Of hatred, and jealous too
Yet we are just friends.

You wished me a happy love life
Said how happy you are
And the tears that you shed
And said were for happiness
Was a lie on my face

We don't talk till late nights
And all you say is how busy you are
You don't say good morning
Giving one excuse after another
But we are just friends

Honestly, do you love me?
Are you jealous of her?
You never ask for my help
You never visit at my place
We are just friends

www.ingramcontent.com/pod-product-compliance
Lightning Source LLC
Chambersburg PA
CBHW050957050726
47592CB00007B/2610